Dopes with the Soap

"Come on, you guys." Nancy reached for the bottle of soap.

Peter tossed it to Jason.

"Give it back, Jason, you big creep!" Bess cried.

Jason threw it to Andrew, and he threw it back to David.

"Soapy-poo, soapy-poo," David called out, holding the bottle above Bess.

David threw the bottle back to Peter. But Peter missed catching it. The bottle hit George's model of the sun and its planets, knocking it to the floor.

The planet Jupiter cracked in half!

The Nancy Drew Notebooks

Available from MINSTREL Books

THE NANCY DREW NOTEBOOKS®

#22

THE CLUE IN THE GLUE

CAROLYN KEENE

Illustrated by Anthony Accardo

A MINSTREL® BOOK

PUBLISHED BY POCKET BOOKS

New York   London   Toronto   Sydney   Tokyo   Singapore

This book is a work of fiction. Names, characters, places, and incidents are products of the author's imagination or are used fictitiously. Any resemblance to actual events or locales or persons living or dead is entirely coincidental.

A MINSTREL PAPERBACK *Original*

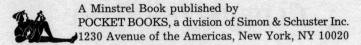

A Minstrel Book published by
POCKET BOOKS, a division of Simon & Schuster Inc.
1230 Avenue of the Americas, New York, NY 10020

Copyright © 1998 by Simon & Schuster Inc.
Produced by Mega-Books, Inc.

ISBN: 0-671-00816-1

First Minstrel Books printing January 1998

10 9 8 7 6 5 4 3 2 1

NANCY DREW, THE NANCY DREW NOTEBOOKS, A MINSTREL BOOK and colophon are registered trademarks of Simon & Schuster Inc.

Cover art by Lina Levy

Printed in the U.S.A.

THE
CLUE IN THE GLUE

1

Soap Bubbles

Pssst! Nancy!" George Fayne pushed a folded piece of paper into Nancy Drew's hand as George walked past Nancy's desk.

Nancy opened the note and read: "Boys are goony loonies." She put her hand over her mouth and tried not to laugh out loud. But a small giggle escaped. Nancy looked up and saw Mrs. Reynolds, her third-grade teacher, staring right at her.

"Nancy and George, you're supposed to be working on the written reports for your science fair projects," Mrs. Reynolds said, "not passing notes to each other."

"Sorry, Mrs. Reynolds," Nancy said softly. She glanced at her best friend. George was connecting an orange Styrofoam ball to her project. It was a model of the solar system. It showed the sun and all its planets.

Nancy looked at the colorful science projects set up on tables along the walls of the classroom. The two third-grade classes at Carl Sandburg Elementary School would be having a mini science fair the next day. Nancy couldn't wait.

"George, I had to speak to you twice last week about passing notes during class," Mrs. Reynolds continued. "I don't want you doing it again. Is that clear?"

George nodded.

"Place your report with your exhibit," Mrs. Reynolds said, "then please return to your desk."

George put her paper down next to her science project. Then she quickly walked back to her desk.

Nancy heard a soft chuckle. She looked over to see Brenda Carlton and Alison Wegman. They were watching George and giggling. Nancy thought Brenda wasn't very nice. She liked to see other kids get in trouble.

The bell rang, signaling the end of school. Mrs. Reynolds stood up from her desk. "Anyone who needs to continue working on his or her science fair project may stay after class."

Some of the students from the other third grade, Mrs. Apple's class, wandered into the room. Students from both classes had been going back and forth for the last few days. They had been looking at the projects as kids were setting them up.

Bess Marvin, George's cousin and Nancy's other best friend, leaned over. She sat across the aisle from Nancy. "We need one more frozen bubble," Bess said. "It should be a really big one."

Nancy and Bess were doing their science fair project together. It showed how to make different soap bubble patterns and how to create frozen soap bubbles in cold weather.

"Okay, Bess, you make one outside, and I'll fix up our display," Nancy said.

She walked over to their project. It was set up on a table by the window. At the next table, Kyle Leddington and Andrew Leoni were working on their magnet project. On the other side, Brenda and Alison had set up their fossil bone display.

Nancy heard Jason Hutchings suddenly call out, "Hey, David, hands off!"

She looked over to where Jason had his invisible ink display. His friend David Berger, who was in Mrs. Apple's class, was playing with the ink on scraps of paper.

"Come on, let me write something with the ink. It's cool," David said as Jason pulled a bottle away from him.

"Go work on your bug project," Jason said.

David and another boy from his class had made a display about cockroaches of the world. Nancy thought it was gross.

Nancy saw Bess come back into the classroom. Bess was walking slowly as she carried a delicate frozen ice bubble that she'd just made outside. She'd blown a large soap bubble and then let it freeze in the cold air. Beautiful ice crystals had formed all over it.

"Ooh, Bess! That's the best one we've made so far!" Nancy said. "Quick, put it in the ice chest before it melts."

"I love making these," Bess said, carefully placing the frozen bubble in a small ice chest. The girls had put ice packs in the bottom to keep the frozen bubbles solid.

"Bess and Nancy, that's a great frozen bubble," Mrs. Reynolds said.

Nancy and Bess beamed with pride.

"Thanks, Mrs. Reynolds," Nancy said.

Their teacher looked around the

room. "As a matter of fact, everyone's display is wonderful," she said. "It will be hard to decide whose is the best."

Mrs. Reynolds and Mrs. Apple were going to judge the science projects the following morning. They would pick a best project from each class. The winners would get first-place ribbons. At the end of the week, both classes were going on a field trip to Chicago. They would visit the Adler Planetarium.

"Okay, everyone should be finishing up," Mrs. Reynolds called out as she walked to the door. "I'll be in the other classroom for a few minutes if anyone needs me."

"Oh, Nancy," Bess said. "My mom pulled into the parking lot while I was outside. She says we have to hurry up because she has to go to the doctor after she drops you and George off."

"Okay, we'd better tell George," Nancy said, looking across the room. "She's still working on her project."

"Hey, George," Nancy called. "Bess's mom is outside. We have to leave."

George nodded, shaking her dark curls. She was attaching the last foam planet to her model. "I'm almost done."

"Hiya, bubble girls," Jason said, walking over to Nancy and Bess's display.

"Ha, ha," Nancy replied.

Jason grinned. "Blowing soap bubbles isn't really science, is it?"

Bess tossed back her long blond hair. "Huh! Your invisible ink isn't science, either. And your ink is stinky."

Jason chuckled. "It's better than a baby bubble project."

"Go drink your invisible ink," Nancy said. She was arranging bottles of soap solution on the table.

"Yeah," Bess added. "Then maybe *you'll* disappear!" The girls giggled.

"Ooh! Inky, dinky, doo." Jason danced around the display table. Suddenly, he grabbed a bottle of soap solution from the table.

"What if I blow some bubbles my-self?" he said, running to the back of the room with the soap bottle.

"Hey, give that back!" Nancy ran after him. Bess was right behind her. Andrew, Kyle, and David also joined in the chase.

Jason stopped by a table near George's display. "David, heads up." Jason tossed David the bottle.

Bess tried to grab it but missed.

"Get it, George!" Nancy called.

George jumped up and tried to get the bottle from David. But he threw it to Peter DeSands.

"Come on, you guys." Nancy reached for the bottle.

Peter tossed it to Jason.

"Give it back, Jason, you big creep!" Bess cried.

Jason threw it to Andrew, and he threw it back to David. The boys were laughing and hollering.

"Soapy-poo, soapy-poo," David called

out, holding the bottle above Bess. She grabbed his arm.

David squirmed away and threw the bottle back to Peter. But Peter missed catching it. The bottle hit George's project, knocking it to the floor.

The planet Jupiter from George's model cracked in half!

2

A Broken Planet

My planet!" George yelled.

Mrs. Reynolds came back into the room. "What's all the shouting about?" she said. "What happened to George's model?"

"David threw the bottle and knocked over George's model!" Nancy cried.

"But it was all Jason's fault. He took the bottle in the first place," Bess added.

Soon everyone was arguing.

"Quiet!" Mrs. Reynolds said. "Now, Jason, why don't you tell me what happened."

"I took their soap bottle," Jason said. "But I didn't mean to hurt anything."

"Jason, you should have been respectful of the girls' projects," Mrs. Reynolds said. She examined the broken piece. "Luckily, this doesn't look too bad. George, I think it can be fixed."

"Sorry your planet got squished," Jason said. "I can glue it for you."

"No way!" George replied. "I don't want you touching my model."

"I'll help George," Nancy offered. She and George picked up the broken model.

"You guys, we really have to leave," Bess said, looking worried. "My mom has an appointment."

Mrs. Reynolds patted George on the back. "You can glue it in the morning."

"Sorry about your model, George," Andrew said as he was leaving the room. "It was neat. I have some glue next to my display if you need it."

George didn't answer. Nancy knew George was mad at *all* the boys. Nancy didn't blame George. She had worked hard on her project.

George had painted different-size Styrofoam balls to make the nine planets and the sun. Then she had put each planet on a stiff wire. The other end of the wires were stuck into the sun. Her dad had helped her make a wooden stand to hold up the sun. The model was cool-looking, Nancy thought. And now it was broken.

The next morning Nancy arrived at school just as Bess and George were getting out of the Marvins' red minivan. "Hi!" Nancy called. "Cute hat, Bess."

Bess had on a pink knit cap with pretty pink and white roses on one side.

"Thanks," Bess said, smiling. "It's part of my new skating outfit."

A group of kids was going to the ice rink after school. Nancy had worn her favorite red-and-white skating sweater with a snowflake pattern on it. She couldn't wait to practice a new spin that she and Bess had learned in their last ice-skating lesson.

The three girls walked toward the school entrance. A group of boys was having a snowball fight on the playground.

Jason yelled to George, "Hey, George! Want a chewy, gooey Jelly Jet?" He waved a small box. Jelly Jets were Jason's favorite candy. They were fruit-flavored jelly candies shaped like jet planes.

"No. Don't think some candy will make me forget about yesterday!" George called, and continued walking. Suddenly, a snowball hit her in the back. The girls spun around as the group of boys began to laugh.

David stood there with a big grin. He raised his hands in the air and tried to look innocent. David gave Mike Minelli and Jason high fives and turned away.

"Watch this," George said. She made a huge snowball, took aim, and threw.

Splat! David jumped as the snowball landed right in the middle of his back.

"Hey!" He turned and looked at George.

George raised her hands in the air, acting innocent, imitating David. "I wonder who threw that?" she said. Nancy, Bess, and George burst into laughter and ran into the school building.

Nancy and Bess tossed their backpacks on their desks and joined George at her display table. She had a puzzled look on her face.

"What's wrong?" Nancy asked.

"Someone glued Jupiter back together." George held up the Styrofoam ball. "Mrs. Reynolds, did you glue my planet?" George asked the teacher.

"No, but Jason and a few other boys were in here earlier," Mrs. Reynolds said. "Maybe one of them did."

"Jason might have fixed it, George," Nancy said. "He said he was really sorry."

George shrugged. "I have to get this planet back on my solar system. I'm going to get some wire from my desk."

"I'll go with you," Bess said.

Nancy moved close to the table to look at George's model. She stepped on something.

It was an empty plastic glue tube. She picked it up. This could be a clue to whoever fixed George's model, Nancy thought.

Then she noticed something white sticking out from under George's model. Putting the glue tube in her pocket, Nancy leaned close to the model. Just then Bess and George came back.

"George, look. There's something under your model." Nancy pointed at the corner.

George pulled out a folded piece of notepaper. It had little smiley faces at the top.

" 'Sorry about your display,' "

George read. She showed the note to Nancy and Bess.

"Hey! We have that same kind of notepaper at my house," Bess said.

"There's no name on it," George said.

"Somebody fixed your model and didn't tell who they were," Nancy said. "Why?"

"I got a note on that same smiley-face paper in my cubby yesterday," George said. "But I thought it was from Bess."

"Me?" Bess looked puzzled. "I didn't leave you a note."

"Wait, I'll get it," George said.

The bell rang for class to begin. Nancy and Bess sat down at their desks along with everyone else. George walked up the aisle to Nancy's desk. She knelt down in the middle of the aisle and showed Bess and Nancy the other smiley-face note.

It said "Hi, George!" Nancy compared it to the note found under

17

George's model. "The printing looks the same on both notes," she said.

"Maybe the person who wrote George this note fixed her model, too," Bess said.

"Maybe." Nancy stared at the notes.

Suddenly, Nancy realized the class was quiet. She looked up. Everyone, including Mrs. Reynolds, was staring at them.

"George, what did I say about passing notes?" Mrs. Reynolds asked.

"I'm not, Mrs. Reynolds," George said. "I was just showing this . . . uh . . ." George paused and looked around at the other kids staring at her.

"I won't tell you again," Mrs. Reynolds said. "No more passing notes during class."

George went to her desk as Mrs. Apple and her third-grade class began to file into the room. Mrs. Reynolds announced that she and Mrs. Apple were going to start looking at the science projects to decide the winners. She invited all the students to look at the projects in the two classrooms.

Mrs. Apple reminded everybody to be quiet as they went from one classroom to the other.

Nancy remembered the glue tube in her pocket. Taking it out, she looked at the tube. She thought about who might have fixed George's model. It certainly was a mystery, she decided.

Nancy liked to solve mysteries, and she was good at solving them, too. The glue tube was a clue, she thought. A good detective always gathers clues.

She tucked the small tube into a plastic pocket in her special blue detective's notebook. Her father had given it to her. Nancy used it when she was solving a mystery.

Nancy joined George and Bess.

"Let's go see the exhibits in the other class," Nancy said. The girls went next door.

"Oh, how cool!" George exclaimed, pointing to a display. "Look at Amara

Shane's plants and water project. Colored celery!"

"That's so fun!" Nancy agreed. The girls walked to another table.

"Yuck! A spider exhibit." Bess shivered. "They give me the creeps."

"Speaking of creeps," George said, "here comes David Berger."

"Hey, George, want to pet Tubby?" David held up a huge dead cockroach.

"Yeeeew! No!" George cried. She jumped back from David and the insect. "Is that from your Cockroaches of the World project?"

"Yep." David grinned proudly. "Come on, give him a chance. Pet little Tubby." He waved the bug at her.

"She said no, so go away!" Nancy cried. "And take your yucky friend with you."

Andrew Leoni was checking out a weather project on a table nearby. Nancy saw him look up at David and George. "Leave George alone," Andrew called.

David shrugged and laughed. "Okay," he said, walking back to his exhibit.

"That was nice of Andrew to stop David from bothering you," Nancy said.

"Yes," George agreed. "He was 'bugging' me!" The three friends giggled.

The girls looked at some more projects. Then they went back to their own classroom. Finally, the teachers said it was time to announce the winners. The students from both third grades crowded into Mrs. Reynolds's classroom.

"The winner from our class," Mrs. Apple said, "is . . . Amara Shane."

"Oh, I'm glad she won," Nancy said, applauding with the rest of the students. "That red celery was cool."

Now the teachers were ready to name the winner from Mrs. Reynolds's class.

"I hope we win, Nancy," Bess said.

"Me, too," Nancy replied. "Cross your fingers for good luck." She held up both hands, fingers crossed.

"Well, we found it very difficult to come to a decision about a winner from this class," Mrs. Reynolds said. "So, finally, we decided it could only be . . ."

Nancy held her breath.

". . . a tie!"

3

Smiley-Face Notes

The winners are George Fayne and Jason Hutchings!" Mrs. Reynolds said. Everyone applauded again.

Nancy was disappointed that she and Bess had lost. She was happy, though, that George had won.

George, Jason, and Amara went to the front to get their blue ribbons. The ribbons had gold lettering that read First Prize.

"After lunch the three winners will present their projects to the two third-grade classes," Mrs. Reynolds said. "If anyone would like to continue to look at the science projects, you have permission to come into the classroom during lunchtime."

Mrs. Apple's class went back to their room.

"Everyone, it's time for lunch," Mrs. Reynolds said. "George, please come see me before you go to the cafeteria."

"I hope George isn't in trouble," Bess said as she and Nancy walked with the rest of the class to the cafeteria.

George arrived at lunch ten minutes late. "Tell us what happened," Nancy said as George put her tray down at their table.

"When I went to put my award ribbon away inside my desk," George explained, "I found a new smiley-face note. Mrs. Reynolds saw me reading it."

"Ooh," Bess said. "Are you in trouble?"

George nodded. "You're not kidding. She thought *I* wrote it and was going to pass it to someone."

Nancy's eyes grew wide. "Uh-oh," she said.

"I tried to tell Mrs. Reynolds that I found it in my desk and I didn't know where it came from."

"Why didn't you just show her the note?" Nancy asked.

"She didn't give me a chance." George paused. "Anyway," she continued, "she didn't believe me when I tried to explain. She said it was bad enough that I ignored her warning to stop passing notes during class. But to make up stories was even worse."

"But you weren't making up stories," Nancy said.

"Mrs. Reynolds thinks I was," George replied.

"What's she going to do?" Bess asked.

"She says she won't let me go on the field trip to the planetarium if she sees me with notes again," George said unhappily.

"Oh, no!" Nancy said. "You have to come!"

"Who won't let you go on the field

trip?" Brenda Carlton walked up to the table.

"Don't be so nosy, Brenda," Bess said.

"Hmm, this sounds like something good for my newspaper," Brenda said.

Brenda had her own newspaper, called the *Carlton News*. She typed it herself, with help from her dad, on a computer at home.

"Mrs. Reynolds hasn't said for sure that George can't go," Nancy said. "You should only print the facts."

"We'll see," Brenda said as she walked away.

"Great. Now Brenda is writing a stupid article about me in her paper." George groaned. "Listen, you guys, I really want to see the new sky show at the planetarium. So, I can't let Mrs. Reynolds see me with another note again," George said to Nancy and Bess. "I have to figure out who's leaving them and get whoever it is to stop."

"We'll help you," Nancy said. "Let's

start right now. First of all, what does the new note say?"

George turned red. She pulled the note from her pocket but kept it in her hand. "The note's right here."

Bess reached for it. "Let's read it." She grabbed the paper, but George grabbed it back.

"George, why won't you show us the note?" Nancy asked. "Bess and I are your best friends."

George slowly slid the note across the table. It was also on smiley-face paper. The two girls read: "George, I think you are pretty." There was a wiggly line under the word "pretty."

Nancy and Bess looked at George, then down again at the note. Nancy's eyes grew wide.

"George, this is from . . . this is from a . . ." Bess couldn't finish because she was laughing so hard. "EEEEeeee-wwww!" she shrieked, and doubled over.

"A *boy* likes George!"

4

Invisible Ink Tricks

Bess, stop it!" George looked around. "I don't want the whole cafeteria to know."

"That you got a note from a boy!" Bess added, still giggling.

"We'll help you," Nancy said. She pulled her detective notebook out of her pocket and opened it. Then she wrote: "Who is sending secret notes to George?"

"Do you have the other two notes?" Nancy asked.

"Yes." George took them from her pocket and placed them on the table.

"So, you got three notes on smiley-face notepaper," Nancy said, writing in her blue notebook.

"And someone fixed my model," George reminded her. "We also have to find out who did that."

"I'm already working on that mystery," Nancy said. She pulled out the empty glue tube she'd put in her blue notebook.

"Where did you get that?" George asked.

Nancy told Bess and George about finding it under the display table. "I think whoever glued your model left it there."

"That's not Glue Boy glue like everyone else in class uses," George said. "It's Peacock's Glue, that pasty stuff."

"Who uses that?" Bess asked.

"I don't know," Nancy said, staring at the tube. "But we'll find out." Nancy wrote again in her notebook: "Who glued the model?" She looked up. "Hey, this is two mysteries rolled into one!"

"Good." Bess clapped her hands.

"Two mysteries in one means we'll solve them both at the same time."

Nancy looked back at the three notes. "The last note says you're pretty." She wrote that in her notebook. "So now we know it's a boy who wrote the notes. Maybe whoever fixed your model was around yesterday after school. Or this morning. It could have been one of the boys."

"Jason was there," Bess said, "and Andrew and David."

George frowned. "It couldn't be David. He's been acting so mean."

"Yeah," Nancy agreed. "Whoever wrote the notes is someone who really likes you."

George's face got red again.

"Well, it's true, George," Nancy said. "Have Andrew or Jason been extra nice to you?"

"No," George said.

"Yes, they have," Bess said. "Remember when Andrew stopped David from waving that gross cockroach at you?"

Nancy nodded. "He also told you he was sorry about your model getting broken. And Jason was, too."

"So, they've both been extra nice," Bess said.

Nancy wrote in her notebook:

<u>Suspects</u>
Andrew
Jason

She looked at the notes again.

"I think we should check out Jason's and Andrew's handwriting. We'll compare it to the notes. Let's look at the reports they had to write for their projects."

"Okay," George said. "Come on."

The three girls finished eating and went back to the classroom. A few other kids were there, along with Mrs. Reynolds.

Nancy spotted Jason. She wondered if he had glued George's model but didn't tell her because he didn't want

George to know he liked her. Nancy had an idea.

"Jason, guess what?" she asked. "Somebody glued the broken piece on George's model before we got to school this morning. Wasn't that nice?" She watched his face.

Jason squinted his eyes. "I guess," he said. Then he shrugged and walked away.

What was that funny look? Nancy wondered.

Nancy joined Bess and George. They were at Kyle and Andrew's magnet exhibit. She told the girls about questioning Jason.

"If he gave you a funny look, I'll bet he did fix George's model," Bess said.

"It's too soon to tell," Nancy replied. "We need more clues to prove it's Jason."

She looked at the printing on the report with Kyle and Andrew's exhibit. Nancy had seen Andrew writing it the day before. She compared the writing to the notes. "Andrew's printing looks kind of like the writing on the notes."

"A little," George said. "Let's look at Jason's writing."

"Jason's sign was made on a computer." Nancy looked across the room at the sign over Jason's display: Think Invisible Ink.

"We'll look at his report," she said.

At Jason's table, they found that his report also had been made on a computer.

"Too bad. I really wanted to compare his writing to the notes," George said.

"We'll check out one of his school papers," Nancy said.

The bell rang, signaling the end of lunch. The students from both third-grade classes came into Mrs. Reynolds's classroom. It was time for the presentations by the winners of the science fair.

Amara Shane went first.

"My project shows how the leaves of plants suck up water through the plant stems," she said. "You can see this if you put celery in water with red food coloring in it. The stems turn red. Neat, huh?" Amara smiled proudly, and everyone applauded.

George went next.

"Our solar system has nine planets, and they circle around the sun," George began. She jiggled her mobile to make the planets move around. "This planet is Mercury," George said, pointing to the planet closest to the sun. She gave a little speech about each planet as she pointed it out on her model. When she was done, she also got a big round of applause.

Finally, it was Jason's turn. First he gave a quick talk about how juice from citrus fruits can work as invisible ink. He explained that grapefruits, oranges, lemons, and limes were all citrus fruits.

"If you put citrus juice on a piece of paper, the juice will turn brown when the paper is held near something hot, like a lightbulb."

Jason took a Q-tip and dipped it in

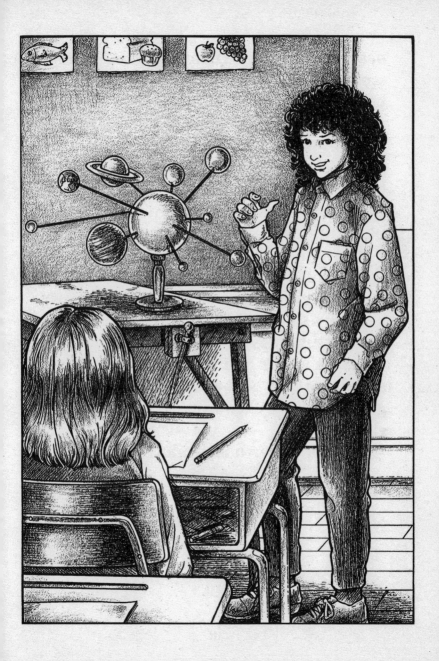

grapefruit juice. Then he wrote some words with the juice on a small piece of paper.

He waved the paper. "The writing is invisible!"

After a minute, Jason held the paper over the bare lightbulb of a desk lamp that Mrs. Reynolds had put on his display table.

"Now the letters are turning brown," Jason announced. He held up the paper to show everyone the words.

Nancy strained to see from where she was sitting. The paper was small, and other students were in the way. She stood up to get a better look, and gasped. Nancy couldn't believe what she saw.

Jason's paper had smiley faces on it!

5

Cheater! Cheater!

Nancy stared at the smiley-face paper.

"Nancy, Jason *must* be the note writer," Bess whispered. "He has smiley-face paper!"

The paper did make Jason look guilty. George turned and stared at Nancy. Nancy wondered if she was thinking the same thing.

"Mrs. Reynolds, no one can see the paper. It's too small," Nancy called out.

Mrs. Reynolds asked Jason to pick someone to make another test on a larger piece of paper. Jason chose David.

David wrote his note, then waved it in the air to dry it fast. Then he held it over the lightbulb.

When the message appeared, he held up the paper for everyone to see. On it he'd written: "Invisible ink is not stinky!" The words "is not" were underlined. David looked at Bess and smiled.

"Ha! He's making fun of what I said to Jason yesterday," Bess said.

Nancy started to move closer to Jason's exhibit table so she could get a look at the smiley-face paper. But Jason stuffed it into his pants pocket. I'll have to figure out a way to look at that piece of paper, Nancy thought.

As Nancy, Bess, and George left school that afternoon, Andrew came up behind them. "I thought your science project was the best," he told George. "You should have won first prize without there being a tie."

"Wow! That was nice of him to say, don't you think?" Nancy asked.

George made a face. "I guess."

"That makes two times Andrew has said nice things to you, George," Bess said.

The three friends walked out to the parking lot. Hannah Gruen, the Drews' housekeeper, was waiting to drive them to the ice rink.

"Hello, girls. How was school?" Hannah asked. They told her about the science fair and George's first prize.

As they drove to the rink, Nancy said, "I was sure Jason was the one who wrote the notes. After what Andrew said to George, now I'm not so sure."

"Well, I am," George said. "Jason has smiley-face paper."

"That's a good clue, but we need more proof," Nancy replied. "Yesterday I saw David Berger playing with the invisible ink at Jason's display table. He could have been using smiley-face paper, too."

"If it was, then Andrew could have taken it from Jason's table," George said.

"Right," Nancy said. "We still need to see Jason's writing and compare it to the notes."

Nancy asked George if she could keep the three notes. She tucked them into her blue detective's notebook. As she did, she noticed the empty tube of glue.

I bet if we find out whose glue this is, we'll find out who fixed George's model *and* who left the notes, Nancy thought.

At the ice-skating rink, Nancy, Bess, and George joined a group of girls that included Brenda and Alison. Nancy was glad to see Amara and Rebecca Ramirez. Rebecca lived near Nancy. They were friends.

"Hi, you guys." Nancy smiled. "This

is going to be fun. There're lots of kids from our class here." Nancy looked at the other groups of skaters. She spotted Jason and a group of third-grade boys across the ice.

Nancy, George, and Bess skated around a small area. Bess and Nancy showed George the new spin they'd learned at their last lesson.

"Hey, not bad for girls," Jason called as he and David skated over to them. A few boys followed. Jason circled the girls really fast before skidding to a stop in front of them.

"Your skating's not so hot," George said. "I bet I could beat you in a race."

"You're on!" Jason said excitedly.

The other kids backed away, clearing a path for the race. George and Jason lined up.

Nancy said, "Ready, set . . . GO!"

Just as George was about to push off, David reached forward and yanked her red hat off her head. George turned for a second, and Jason got a head start.

"Go, George, go!" Bess screamed.

George took off across the ice. But she couldn't catch up to Jason. He won easily.

"Cheater!" George yelled at Jason. She skated back and grabbed her hat from David.

"No fair!" Nancy called.

"I'm going to get you, David!" George cried. She skated after him. A group of kids followed, and pretty soon the girls were chasing the boys.

Nancy started after Jason. She skated faster and caught up to him. She spotted a piece of paper sticking out of his pants pocket. Maybe that's the paper he used for the invisible ink test, Nancy thought.

"Hey, Jason, what's that in your pocket?" she asked.

"It's the ink test I did at school." Jason waved the paper in the air.

"Oh, your invisible ink was so cool. Can I see it?" Nancy asked sweetly.

"Okay," Jason said. He began to

skate backward and held out the paper. "Come get it," he said with a laugh.

Nancy skated after Jason and managed to grab a corner of the paper. Just then Jason pulled his hand away.

"Don't!" Nancy called.

But it was too late. Jason pulled his hand away. The paper ripped in half!

6

The Smell Will Tell

Nancy was so surprised that she dropped the piece of paper she was holding. She scrambled to pick it up before it fell on the ice, but she wasn't quick enough.

"Oops! Sorry, Nancy," Jason said, skating away.

George and Bess skated up, and Nancy explained what happened. The girls tried to read the wet piece of paper, but the ink had run.

Finally, Nancy sighed. "It's no use. We'll have to look at something else Jason wrote."

On the ride home, Nancy pulled her

47

blue notebook out of her backpack and looked at the names of the two main suspects: Andrew, Jason. She thought about the empty glue tube again.

"Do you guys remember seeing Andrew or Jason with glue yesterday?" Nancy asked.

"Jason offered to glue George's display," Bess said.

"Andrew also offered me glue, remember?" George said.

"We should try to find out tomorrow if they still have their glue," Nancy said.

"If one of them is missing his glue," George said, "that could be who glued my model and left the empty glue tube."

"That's right," Nancy said.

When Nancy arrived at school the next morning, Brenda was handing out the latest issue of the *Carlton News*.

"It's got a juicy article about George," Brenda announced.

"It's a dumb story," George said.

"Is not," Brenda said.

Just then the bell rang for class.

Mrs. Reynolds began class with a spelling lesson. She chose Jason to come to the blackboard to write some words. Good, Nancy thought. Now we can see his writing.

Jason printed on the board.

Bess leaned across the aisle and whispered, "I don't think it looks like the notes, do you?"

Nancy shook her head. Jason's printing didn't exactly match the notes.

After spelling, Mrs. Reynolds announced they would have a special art period. The class was going to make fancy book covers for their reports on the field trip to the planetarium. They were going to glue colored paper cutouts onto the covers.

"We can see what kind of glue Andrew and Jason use," Nancy whispered to Bess.

Nancy walked up to the front to get some colored paper from Mrs. Reynolds's desk. As she passed George's desk, George tugged on her sleeve.

"Nancy!" George whispered. "I got another note." George pointed to her lap. Nancy saw a small piece of folded paper and a Jelly Jet candy.

"Did you get the Jelly Jet with it?" Nancy asked, looking up to make sure Mrs. Reynolds wasn't watching them.

"Yes," George answered.

Jelly Jets are Jason's favorite candy, Nancy thought.

"And, Nancy, this note has no writing on it," George said.

"George Fayne!" Mrs. Reynolds's stern voice rang out.

Nancy and George looked up.

"Are you passing notes again?" Mrs. Reynolds said. "After what I said yesterday?"

"No, Mrs. Reynolds. I—" George tried to explain.

"That's it," Mrs. Reynolds said angrily. "I'm sorry, George. You may not go on the field trip tomorrow."

The class grew very quiet.

George's lower lip started to shake.

"And, Nancy, you are very close to not going also," Mrs. Reynolds said. "Please get back to your desk."

At lunchtime Nancy, Bess, and George went to the cafeteria.

"Mrs. Reynolds is calling my mom to tell her I can't go on the field trip," George said, her eyes filling with tears.

Nancy put an arm around her friend. "George, we'll find out who's writing the notes."

"It'll be too late," George said.

"No, it won't. We can still solve this case," Nancy said. "Did either of you notice anything during art?"

"I heard Jason ask Kyle if he could borrow some glue," Bess said.

"And Andrew had some Glue Boy glue," Nancy added. She took out her detective notebook.

"Andrew's writing didn't match the notes," she said. "We should cross him off as a suspect." She put a line through his name. Under Jason's name, she wrote:

Clues
Smiley-face paper
Jelly Jets
Glue

"George, can I look at the note you got this morning?" Nancy asked. She took a bite of her cream cheese and raisin sandwich.

"You mean the not-note," George said with a laugh. "There was nothing on it." She put down her apple juice carton and dug a piece of paper out of her pants pocket.

Nancy looked at the piece of paper. It was blank except for a yellow smiley face at the top. Nancy noticed that the paper had a faint smell. She sniffed the paper. The smell seemed familiar, but she couldn't think what it was.

This could be another clue, she decided. "Can I borrow this for a while, George?" Nancy asked.

"It's all yours," George said.

"Thanks," Nancy said, and she tucked the note into her blue notebook.

After school Mrs. Marvin picked up Bess and Nancy. George and her mom had to meet with Mrs. Reynolds.

"Nancy, let's get George a present," Bess suggested on the drive home. "To cheer her up."

Nancy grinned. "Good idea."

Bess's mom said she would take them both to the mall after dinner. Mrs. Marvin said they would pick Nancy up at six-thirty.

"See ya later, alligator." Nancy waved after Bess and her mom dropped her off.

"After a while, crocodile," Bess called as they drove away.

Nancy's dog, Chocolate Chip, greeted her at the door. Chip was a brown Labrador retriever.

"Hi, Chip." Nancy patted her puppy's

head. She put down her backpack and went to the kitchen to get some juice.

"There's no apple juice left, Hannah," Nancy said, peering into the refrigerator.

Hannah looked up from making supper. "I think there's some grapefruit juice in the back of the fridge."

"Ugh." Nancy didn't like grapefruit juice very much. But she was thirsty, so she got out the carton and poured herself a glass.

She took out her detective's notebook and put it on the kitchen table. Nancy sat sipping quietly, looking over her clues and thinking.

Nancy took another sip of her drink. Suddenly, she sniffed the juice. There is something familiar about that smell, she thought.

She took out the blank note and smelled it.

"I've got it!" Nancy said excitedly. "The blank note smells like grapefruit juice—just like Jason's invisible ink!"

7

Art Store Surprise

Come on, Chip, we have to test this paper," Nancy said. "I'll bet there's writing on it!"

Nancy rushed up to her bedroom. She took the shade off the table lamp beside her bed. Then she held the blank paper over the lighted bulb. In a minute, words appeared: "I like you." There was a wiggly line under the words.

Nancy pulled out her blue notebook and looked at the other notes. The writing in all the notes looked like the invisible ink note.

Nancy looked at one of the notes

closely: "George, I think you are pretty." There was a wiggly line under the word "pretty."

"Mmm, a wiggly line in two notes. Hey, I've seen this wiggly line under words in something else," Nancy said to Chip. "But where?"

Under Jason's name, she added "Invisible ink note" to the other clues.

"Hi, Pudding Pie." Nancy's father, Carson Drew, came into her room and kissed the top of her head. "What's up?"

"Hi, Daddy. I'm working on a mystery." Nancy gave him a big hug and told him all about George and the notes.

"I'm sure it's Jason," Nancy said. She held out the invisible ink note. "Just look at this note. Jason had an invisible ink project for the science fair."

"Well, if you think all of your clues add up, then you are probably right," Mr. Drew said, winking at Nancy as he

left the room. "But it's always good to double-check your clues."

Nancy flopped down on her bed. "I can't wait to tell George about my clue. I'll call her right now."

After dinner, Bess and her mother picked up Nancy. As they drove to the mall, Nancy told Bess about the invisible ink note.

"George was really excited when I told her, Bess."

"That's super!" Bess said. "Now what do we do?"

"George should talk to Jason and make him go with her to Mrs. Reynolds," Nancy said. "He can tell her that he was writing notes to George, and she didn't know about it. Then she can go on the field trip."

"Let's still get George a present," Bess said.

At the mall, Nancy and Bess went to George's favorite store, Nature Time.

There were so many choices, they couldn't decide what to buy.

"How about a T-shirt that says Save the Tree Frogs?" Nancy asked.

"She might croak over that," Bess said. Then she and Nancy giggled.

"Oh, look. Glow-in-the-dark stars," Nancy said. "She can put them on her ceiling."

After Nancy and Bess paid for the gift, Mrs. Marvin and the girls headed for the front entrance of the mall. On the way, they passed the art supply store.

Jason and David were just leaving the store with their mothers. "Hi, you guys!" Jason called.

Nancy noticed that Jason and David each held a bag. "What did you buy?"

"Just some glue," Jason replied. He pulled out a bottle of Glue Boy.

Then David took out a tube of Peacock's Glue. That's the same glue I found under George's display table! Nancy thought.

"I've never used that glue," Nancy said to David. "Is it good?"

"It's great," David replied. He held up the tube for them to see. "My dad and I use it when we make wood gliders. It's like paste. Real thick and sticky."

"Do you use it for school?" Nancy asked.

"Sure," David said. "It works on paper, too."

"We'd better go, girls," Mrs. Marvin said.

"See ya," Bess called as she and Nancy followed Mrs. Marvin to the main entrance of the mall.

"Are you sure Jason is the one writing George notes?" Bess asked as they rode home. "Maybe it's David."

Nancy wasn't so sure. "I don't know, but all the clues point to Jason."

"Well, it's David who uses the kind of glue you found under George's table," Bess said.

"That's true," Nancy said.

* * *

When Nancy got home, she put on her favorite nightgown with red and pink roses. Chocolate Chip lay curled up in a ball on the floor beside her bed.

Nancy got on top of the bed and opened her blue notebook.

She thought out loud about David.

"I did see David at Jason's display table. He was playing with the invisible ink on some paper. It could have been smiley-face paper, Chip." Nancy gave her puppy a rub behind his ears. Chip thumped her tail on the carpet.

"David does like Jelly Jets. He and Jason are always eating them. And David uses Peacock's Glue." Nancy tapped her pen on her notebook.

"But what about the invisible ink note?"

Nancy studied the notes again. Suddenly, she jumped off the bed. Chip hopped up from the floor, wagging her tail back and forth.

"Chip, that's it!" Nancy picked up

the two notes with wiggly lines in them.

"The wiggly line!" Nancy waved the notes in the air and did a little dance. "I know where I saw it before!" Chocolate Chip jumped around her feet.

"And I know who wrote George's notes and fixed her model!"

8

Boys, Boys, Boys

Nancy woke up extra early the next morning, and Hannah drove her to school.

"Have fun on your field trip today," Hannah said as Nancy hopped out of the car.

"I will, Hannah." Nancy gave her a kiss goodbye. I hope George gets to go, Nancy thought.

Nancy hurried to the classroom and over to Jason's display table. She found the test paper that David had written: "Invisible ink is not stinky!" There was a wiggly line under the words "is not."

"I knew it!" Nancy said right out

loud. "That's where I saw the wiggly line before." Nancy pulled the other notes from her blue notebook. She held two of them near the invisible ink test.

Just like the one under the words in these two notes, she thought. David is the one who wrote the notes!

When George and Bess arrived, Nancy told them what she'd figured out.

"I can't believe it's David," George said. "He's been so mean to me."

The girls left the classroom and found David in front of the school. They marched over to him. "You're writing George secret notes, aren't you?" Nancy asked. "And you're using Jason's smiley-face notepaper."

"I don't know what you're talking about," David said. Nancy thought he looked very nervous.

"Did you fix my model?" George demanded.

David shook his head, but his face got red. Finally, he said, "I might have.

And maybe I left you a note or two. But I was just kidding around."

"George got in trouble because of your notes," Nancy said.

"Yeah, she can't go on the field trip because Mrs. Reynolds caught her reading one of your notes," Bess added.

David looked embarrassed.

"I want you to stop leaving me notes, David," George said. "And I don't want the other kids to know you were sending me notes."

"Neither do I!" David said quickly. "That's why I left you an invisible ink note."

George looked puzzled.

"After Brenda wrote in her paper about you," David explained, "I thought that someone might find one of the notes and read it."

"The way we did," Nancy added.

David nodded. "So, I decided to write in invisible ink."

"David, please don't send me any

more notes, in regular *or* invisible ink!"
George cried.

"Okay," David said. "I gotta go." He turned and ran inside the school building.

Nancy handed George the notes. "We have to talk to Mrs. Reynolds so you can go on the field trip."

"What if she still doesn't believe me?" George asked.

"We can prove David wrote the notes," Nancy replied. "We can show her the handwriting."

"I wish she didn't have to know it's a boy writing me notes. It's so yucky," George said.

The three girls walked back to the classroom to see Mrs. Reynolds. George showed her the written notes and explained about David.

When George finished, Mrs. Reynolds said, "I already knew about the notes."

Nancy, George, and Bess opened their mouths in surprise.

"David just told me a few minutes

ago," the teacher explained. "He told me he'd left some unsigned notes in your desk. He seemed terribly upset that I decided not to let you go on the field trip."

Mrs. Reynolds held out the notes. "It seems David has a crush on you."

George's face turned red.

Mrs. Reynolds put her arm around George's shoulders. "It's okay. I won't tell anybody."

George sighed with relief.

"I'm sorry I didn't believe you, George," Mrs. Reynolds said. "But if you hadn't been passing notes in class those other times, it would have been easier to believe you."

George looked down at the ground.

"You *will* be going on the field trip." Mrs. Reynolds smiled again. "I've already called your mother."

Nancy, Bess, and George cheered.

Later that afternoon Nancy, George, and Bess hunched down low in their theater seats. They were at the Adler Planetarium, waiting for the sky show to begin.

"Isn't this place great?" Bess said.

"Yeah. Look at the neat stars on the ceiling," George said. "Just like the cool glow-in-the-dark stars that I'll be able to put on the ceiling of my bedroom." She smiled at Nancy and Bess, who beamed back.

That night Nancy snuggled down in her bed. Chocolate Chip was fast asleep on the floor. Nancy got out her blue notebook and began to write:

We had a great trip to the planetarium today. It was so much fun. The volcano display was my favorite. The red-hot lava was neat and scary. The sky show was really cool.

Nancy drew a little picture of a volcano in her notebook.

The mystery of George's secret note writer has been solved. It was David Berger. George and I have to remember not to pass notes in class anymore!

Nancy thought about how Jason was a really nice boy after all. So was Andrew. Then she thought about David. He really liked George, but he had been mean to her all week. She wrote:

I've decided that some boys can be pretty nice. Except when they *really* like you. Then they just get weird. Case closed.

BRAND-NEW SERIES!

Meet up with suspense and mystery in

#1 The Gross Ghost Mystery
Frank and Joe are making friends and meeting monsters!

#2 The Karate Clue
Somebody's kicking up a major mess!

#3 First Day, Worst Day
Everybody's mad at Joe! Is he a tattletale?

#4 Jump Shot Detectives
He shoots! He scores! He steals!

By Franklin W. Dixon
Look for a brand-new story every other month
at your local bookseller

A MINSTREL® BOOK

Published by Pocket Books

1398-03